The little Witch

The little Witch was only a hundred and
twenty-seven years old. That's not at all old for a
witch. She spent about six hours a day doing
exercises in witchcraft, but she couldn't get
her spells right. Then she got into deep disgrace
at the Walpurgis Night party. She was given a
year to make herself into a good witch or be
expelled. So many strange and funny things
happened to her in that year that sometimes she
thought she would never pass the test.

Also in Knight Books
by Otfried Preussler

THE LITTLE GHOST
THE LITTLE WATER SPRITE

The Little Witch

Otfried Preussler

Translated by Anthea Bell
Illustrated by Winnie Gayler

KNIGHT BOOKS
Hodder and Stoughton

First published in 1958 by
K. Thienemanns Verlag Stuttgart under
the title of *Die Kleine Hexe*
First published in this translation in
1961 by Abelard-Schuman Ltd

This edition first published in 1973 by
Knight Books
Twelfth impression 1987

Printed and bound in Great Britain
for Hodder and Stoughton
Paperbacks, a division of Hodder and
Stoughton Ltd., Mill Road,
Dunton Green, Sevenoaks, Kent
TN13 2YA.
(Editorial Office: 47 Bedford Square,
London WC1B 3DP) by
Cox & Wyman Ltd., Reading

ISBN 0 340 16704 1

Contents

The little Witch in a temper

Once upon a time there was a little witch who was only a hundred and twenty-seven years old. That's not at all old for a witch.

She lived in a witch's house that stood all alone in the middle of a wood. As she was only a little witch, her witch's house was not particularly big either. But it was big enough for the little Witch; she couldn't have wished for a better house. It had a funny crooked roof, and a twisted chimney, and rickety shutters. There was a baking oven built on to the back of the house. Of course there had to be an oven – a witch's house without one wouldn't be a proper witch's house.

The little Witch had a talking raven. This raven was called Abraxas. He didn't just know how to croak 'Good morning!' and 'Good evening!' like an ordinary raven who has learnt to talk. Abraxas could say anything at all. The little Witch thought a great deal of him, because he was a remarkably wise raven and always spoke his mind to her without mincing matters.

The little Witch spent about six hours a day doing exercises in witchcraft. Witchcraft isn't easy. If you want to get anywhere with witchcraft it's no good being lazy. First you have to learn all the smaller spells and charms, and later on the big ones. You have to study the Book of Witchcraft page by page without skipping a single exercise.

The little Witch had only reached page two hundred and thirteen of the Book of Witchcraft. She was just trying rain making. She was sitting on the seat in front of the oven, with the Book of Witchcraft on her knees, casting spells. Abraxas the raven sat beside her. He was not happy.

'You're supposed to be making it rain,' he croaked reproachfully, 'and what really happens? First of all you make it rain white mice. Then you make it rain frogs. And the third time, fir cones. I can't wait to see if you're going to make it rain properly this time, at least.'

For the fourth time the little Witch tried to make it rain. She made a cloud climb up in the sky, beckoned it nearer, and when it was right overhead she called, 'Rain!'

The cloud opened – and it rained buttermilk!

'Buttermilk!' screeched Abraxas. 'It seems to me you've gone completely crazy. What kind of rain will you make next? Clothes lines? Shoe nails? It might at least be breadcrumbs or raisins!'

'I must have made a mistake in the spell,' said the little Witch. She had done that before sometimes. But four times in a row?

'Made a mistake!' croaked Abraxas the raven. 'I'll tell you what the matter is. You're not concentrating. If you keep thinking about other things while you cast spells, of course you make mistakes. You want to concentrate a bit more.'

'Do you think so?' asked the little Witch. Suddenly she shut the Book of Witchcraft with a bang. 'You're right!' she cried angrily. 'It's quite true, I'm not concentrating. And why not?' She glared defiantly at the raven. 'Because I'm furious!'

'Furious?' repeated Abraxas the raven. 'What about?'

'It's Walpurgis Night today, that's why I'm in a bad temper,' said the little Witch. 'All the witches meet today at the dance on the Brocken mountain!'

'Well?'

'And the big witches say I'm still too small for the witches' dance. They don't want me to ride to the mountain and dance with them.'

'Well now,' said the raven, trying to comfort the little Witch, 'you can't expect the big witches to think you old enough at a hundred and twenty-seven. It will all come right once you're older.'

'Humph!' said the little Witch. 'But I want to join in this time, do you hear?'

'It's no use fretting for what you can't get,' croaked the raven. 'Does being angry make any difference? Be sensible! What can you do about it?'

'I know what I'm going to do about it,' said the little Witch. 'I'm going to ride to the Brocken mountain tonight.'

The raven was horrified.

'To the mountain! – But the big witches have forbidden you to go! They'll be having their witches' dance.'

'Bah!' cried the little Witch. 'Lots of things are forbidden. But if you don't get caught –'

'They will catch you!' the raven prophesied.

'Nonsense!' she answered. 'I shan't join the other witches until they're in the middle of the dance – and I shall ride home again before it's over. I shan't be noticed in the confusion on the mountain tonight.'

Hurrah for Walpurgis Night!

The little Witch was not going to let Abraxas the raven frighten her. That night she rode to the Brocken mountain.

All the big witches had met there already. They were dancing round the bonfire, their hair flying and their skirts fluttering. There were perhaps five or six hundred witches, all told: mountain-witches, wood-witches, marsh-witches, mist-witches and storm-witches, wind-witches, flower-witches and herb-witches. They swirled in wild confusion, waving their broomsticks.

'Walpurgis Night! Hurrah for Walpurgis Night!' sang the witches. From time to time they bleated, crowed and screeched; they made thunder roll and lightning flash.

The little Witch mingled unnoticed with the dancers. 'Hurrah for Walpurgis Night!' she sang at the top of her voice. She whirled round the bonfire with the others. 'If Abraxas could see me now he'd open his eyes as wide as an owl,' she thought to herself.

And no doubt everything else would have gone smoothly too – if only the little Witch hadn't had to dance right into her aunt, Rumpumpel the storm-witch. Aunt Rumpumpel couldn't take a joke. She was cross and conceited.

'Well now, what a surprise!' she cried when the little Witch met her in the crowd. 'What are you doing here? Answer me! Don't you know young people are forbidden to come to the Brocken mountain tonight?'

'Don't give me away!' begged the little Witch in dismay.

'Nonsense!' replied Aunt Rumpumpel. 'You must be punished, you impudent little thing.'

The other witches came up, full of curiosity, and surrounded the two of them. Angrily the storm-witch explained. Then she asked what should be done to the little Witch.

'She must pay for it!' cried the mist-witches.

'To the Head Witch with her!' screeched the mountain-witches. 'To the Head Witch, this minute!'

'Yes, yes!' shouted all the witches. 'Seize her and bring her to the Head Witch!'

The little Witch begged and prayed in vain. Aunt Rumpumpel took her by the collar and dragged her before the Head Witch. The Head Witch was squatting on a throne made of pronged pokers. She

frowned as she listened to the storm-witch. Then she
thundered at the little Witch.

'How dare you ride to the Brocken mountain tonight, when it's forbidden for witches of your age?
Where did you get this crazy idea?'

'I don't know,' said the little Witch, trembling with
fright. 'Suddenly I did so want to – and then I think I
jumped on my broomstick and rode here . . .'

'Then kindly ride home again!' the Head Witch

ordered her. 'Be off, as quick as you can. Or I might
lose my temper.'

At this the little Witch saw that she could venture

to talk to the Head Witch. 'Then at least may I come and join the dancing next year?' she asked.

'Hm . . .' The Head Witch thought it over. 'I can't make any promises today. If you've been a good witch all the year – then perhaps . . . I'll call a council of witches the day before next Walpurgis Night, and then I'll give you a test. But it won't be an easy test.'

'Oh, thank you, thank you!' said the little Witch.

She promised to be a good witch till next year. Then she leapt on her broomstick ready to ride home. But then Rumpumpel the storm-witch asked the Head Witch,

'Aren't you going to punish the impudent little creature?'

'Yes, punish her!' the other storm-witches demanded.

'Punish her!' cried all the rest. 'We must keep the rules. A witch who rides to the dance without permission must be punished.'

'We could throw the naughty little toad in the fire a bit, for a punishment,' said Aunt Rumpumpel.

'Suppose we locked her up for a few weeks?' suggested a flower-witch. 'I've got an empty goose-coop at home . . .'

'I've got a better idea,' said a marsh-witch. 'Give her to me. I'll put her in a mudhole up to her neck.'

'No,' the herb-witches contradicted her. 'We ought to give her face a good scratching.'

'Scratch her too!' spat the wind-witches. 'But she deserves a beating as well!'

'With willow-wands!' hissed the mountain-witches.

'Use the broomstick!' Aunt Rumpumpel suggested.

The little Witch was terrified. Suppose it really happened?

'Attention!' said the Head Witch, when all the other witches had spoken. 'If you insist on punishing the little Witch –'

'We do!' shouted the witches in chorus. Aunt Rumpumpel shouted loudest of all.

'Then here's my decision,' said the Head Witch. 'We'll just take away her broomstick and send her home on foot. It will take her three days and nights to get back to her wood – that's enough.'

'It's not enough!' shrieked Rumpumpel the storm-witch. But the others agreed that that would do. They took the little Witch's broomstick away from her, threw it on the fire with howls of laughter, and spitefully wished her a good journey.

Plans for revenge

It was a long, weary way back. It took the little Witch three days and three nights. She came home on the morning of the fourth day with sore feet and holes in her shoes.

'Thank goodness you're back at last!' Abraxas the raven welcomed her. He had been sitting on the chimney of the witch's house keeping an anxious watch for her. When he caught sight of the little Witch a weight fell from the raven's mind. He spread his wings and flew to meet her.

'This is a fine way to behave!' he scolded. 'Gadding all over the place for days on end while I sit helpless at home!' He hopped from one leg to the other. 'You look dreadful! Covered with dust from head to foot! And why are you limping? Did you walk? I thought you had your broomstick with you!'

'I did!' sighed the little Witch.

'I did?' croaked Abraxas. 'What does that mean?'

'It means it's gone.'

'Your broomstick . . .?'

'Gone,' the little Witch repeated.

Light began to dawn on the raven. He put his head on one side and said,

'So they caught you, then? Only to be expected. I should have been much surprised if they hadn't caught you! Well, you deserved all you got.'

It was all the same to the little Witch. 'Sleep!' she thought. 'Oh, for some sleep!' She limped into the bedroom and fell on top of the bed.

'Hi!' cried Abraxas, shocked. 'Aren't you even going to take your dirty clothes off?'

But she was already snoring.

She slept like a top till late next morning. When she woke up Abraxas was perching on her bedpost.

'Had your sleep out?'

'Just about,' said the little Witch, yawning.

'Well, now might I hear what happened?'

'Breakfast first!' the little Witch grumbled. 'I can't talk on an empty stomach.'

She had a long, satisfying breakfast. When she was so full she couldn't have eaten another mouthful, she pushed her plate away and explained.

'Well, you've had a lucky escape, for all your rashness,' said the raven when she had told her story. 'Now, don't you forget to be a good witch till next year.'

'I'll take great care,' she promised. 'I'll work seven hours a day instead of six from now on. And I've something else to do, too – something just as important.'

'What?'

The little Witch made a face. She looked very fierce. Then she explained, saying each word clearly,

'I – will – be – re-venged!'

'On whom?'

'On Aunt Rumpumpel. It's all her fault, the beast! She gave me away to the other witches, she did! I've got her to thank for my sore feet and worn-out shoes!

Who stirred up the others against me? Who was the first to say the Head Witch must punish me? She wasn't even satisfied with burning my broomstick. She still kept on at me.'

'That was really mean of her, certainly,' said the raven. 'But revenge . . .?'

'I'll bewitch her! I'll give her a pig's snout!' hissed the little Witch. 'And donkey's ears! And calf's feet! A goat's beard on her chin – and a cow's tail hanging on behind!'

'Cow's tail? Goat's beard?' said Abraxas discouragingly. 'As if you could annoy old Rumpumpel like that! She's a witch the same as you – she'll bewitch it all away again in a twinkling!'

'Do you think so?' – The little Witch realized that a donkey's ears and calf's feet were no use this time. 'Never mind!' she replied. 'I expect I shall think up something better! Something that will be a match even for Aunt Rumpumpel. Do you think I shall?'

'It's possible,' answered Abraxas. 'Only I'm afraid you'll be very sorry for it if you do hurt Rumpumpel the storm-witch.'

'Why?' asked the little Witch, puzzled.

'Because you promised the Head Witch to be a *good* witch. And if you ask me, good witches aren't supposed to hurt people. Get that into your head.'

The little Witch looked doubtfully at the raven.

'Do you mean that?'

'Certainly I do,' said Abraxas. 'I'd think it over, if I were you.'

Do you sell brooms?

What does a little Witch do for sore feet? She brews
an ointment of toad-spawn and mouse-droppings,
stirs in a handful of ground bats' teeth and lets it cook
through on the open fire. When she spreads this ointment on the sore places, muttering a spell out of the
Book of Witchcraft at the same time, her feet heal in a
few minutes.

'There, that's all right!' said the little Witch in
relief, when the spell and the ointment had done their
work.

'Don't you have to limp any more now?' asked
Abraxas.

'See for yourself!' cried the little Witch. She danced
barefoot round the witch's house. Then she put on her
shoes and stockings.

'Are you going out?' asked the raven in surprise.

'Yes. You can come too,' said the little Witch. 'I'm
going to the village.'

'It's a long way,' said Abraxas. 'Don't forget you've
lost your broomstick; you'll have to walk.'

'That's the point. I don't want to have to walk any

more. So as I don't want to walk any more, I've got to walk into the village.'

'Are you making fun of me?'

'Why? I want to buy a broomstick, if you don't mind. That's all.'

'That's different,' said Abraxas. 'Of course I'll come too. Or you might go staying away for ages again!'

The path to the village went right through the wood, over gnarled roots and broken rocks, fallen trees and slopes covered with brambles. That didn't worry Abraxas the raven much. He sat on the little Witch's shoulder, and all he had to do was to take care that a branch didn't hit him unexpectedly on the head. But the little Witch kept stumbling over roots and catching her clothes on the twigs.

'What a dreadful path!' she said time and again. 'I shall be able to ride again soon, that's the only comfort.'

They reached the village and went to see the shopkeeper, Baldwin Peppercorn. Mr Peppercorn thought little of it when the little Witch and her raven came in at the door. He had never seen a witch before, so he took her for just an ordinary little old woman from one of the nearby villages.

They wished each other good day. 'What can I do for you?' Mr Peppercorn asked kindly.

First the little Witch bought a quarter of a pound of

peppermints. Then she held the bag under the raven's beak, saying, 'Help yourself!'

'Thank you very much!' croaked Abraxas.

Mr Peppercorn was most surprised. 'What a clever bird!' he said in admiration. 'What else would you like?' he went on.

'Do you sell brooms and brushes?' asked the little Witch.

'Certainly!' said Mr Peppercorn. 'Handbrushes, kitchen brushes, birch brooms. And scrubbing brushes too, of course. Or perhaps you wanted a feather whisk . . .

'No thank you, I want a birch broom.'

'With or without broomstick?'

'With a stick,' said the little Witch. 'The stick is the most important part. But it mustn't be too short.'

'How about this one here?' Mr Peppercorn suggested helpfully. 'I'm afraid brooms with longer sticks are out of stock just now.'

'I think it's long enough,' said the little Witch. 'I'll take it.'

'Shall I wrap the broom up?' asked Mr Peppercorn. 'It will be easier to carry if I put a bit of string round it.'

'That's very kind of you,' said the little Witch. 'But it doesn't need wrapping up.'

'Just as you like.' Mr Peppercorn counted out the change and showed the little Witch to the door. 'Good day, I am your most obedi-ent – '

'Servant,' he was just going to add. But what he saw took his breath away.

He saw his customer put the broomstick between her legs. She muttered something, and whoosh! away flew the broomstick carrying her and the raven.

Mr Peppercorn couldn't believe his eyes.

'Heaven help me!' he thought. 'Can queer things like that really happen – or am I dreaming?'

Good resolutions

The little Witch hurtled away on her new broomstick like a whirlwind in human form. She tore over the roofs and gables of the village, her hair streaming and her kerchief fluttering. Abraxas perched on her shoulder, clinging on for dear life.

'Look out!' he croaked suddenly. 'The church tower!'

The Little Witch was only just in time to turn the broomstick aside. A shade closer, and she would have been left hanging on top of the tower. Only her apron caught on the beak of the iron weathercock. Rip! it tore in two.

'Fly slower!' scolded the raven. 'You'll break your neck rushing along like this. Have you gone mad?'

'It's not me,' cried the little Witch. 'It's the broomstick. It's running away with me, the brute!'

New broomsticks are just like young horses. You have to start by taming them and breaking them in. You can count yourself lucky to get off with nothing worse than a torn apron.

But the little Witch was cunning. She steered the

broomstick as well as she could out into the open
fields. She couldn't bump into anything there. 'Now,
you buck!' she told the broomstick. 'Just you buck!
When you've tired yourself out you'll see reason all
right! Gee-up!'

The broomstick tried every imaginable way of
throwing her. It leapt wildly in all directions, it reared
up and let itself drop down – it was no use. The little
Witch sat firm. She couldn't be shaken off.

At last the broomstick gave up. It was worn out. Now it obeyed the little Witch's slightest command. Obediently it flew now fast, now slow, straight forward or round in a curve.

'There now!' said the little Witch contentedly. 'Why couldn't you do that to begin with?'

She straightened her clothes and her kerchief. Then she gave the broomstick a blow with the flat of her hand – and they flew gently towards the wood.

The new broomstick had become as gentle as a lamb. They sailed over the tops of trees, looking down at the rocks and brambles far below. Happily the little Witch let her legs dangle. She was glad she wouldn't have to get about on foot any more. She waved to the hares and deer she saw in the thickets, and counted the foxholes.

'Look there – a huntsman!' croaked Abraxas the raven after a time, pointing down with his beak.

'I see him,' said the little Witch. She pursed her lips and spat, right on top of the huntsman's hat.

'What did you do that for?' asked Abraxas.

'Because it's a good joke!' she chuckled. 'Ha, ha! He'll think it's raining!'

The raven was not amused. 'That's wrong,' he said severely. Good witches don't spit on people's hats.'

'Oh, shut up!' she said angrily.

'Thank you very much,' croaked Abraxas, hurt.

'But Aunt Rumpumpel will laugh up her sleeve at your "jokes".'

'The storm-witch ... What's it got to do with *her*?'

'A great deal,' said the raven. 'Don't you think she'll be pleased if you've failed to be a good witch all the year? Are you going to give her that satisfaction?'

The little Witch shook her head vigorously.

'All the same, unless I'm much mistaken, you're well on the way to do it,' Abraxas told her. He said no more. The little Witch was silent too. What Abraxas had said made her think. She brooded over it gloomily. But however she looked at it, the raven was still right. When they got home she said,

'Yes, that's true. I *must* be a good witch. It's the only way to pay out that Rumpumpel. I'll make her turn green and yellow for fury!'

'So you will!' croaked Abraxas. 'But from now on you really must do nothing but good.'

'I won't fail!' she promised.

Whirlwind

So from then on the little Witch studied her Book of Witchcraft seven hours a day instead of six. By next Walpurgis Night she meant to know everything a good witch could be expected to know. She was still young enough to learn easily; soon she could cast all the important spells from memory.

In between whiles she sometimes went out for a ride. She needed a change after so many hours of hard practice. It even happened, since she had bought her new broomstick, that she went walking in the wood now and then. *Choosing* to walk is not at all the same thing as *having* to walk.

One day, when she was wandering about the wood with Abraxas the raven, she met three old women. All three carried baskets on their backs, and they were peering at the ground as if they were looking for something.

'What are you looking for?' asked the little Witch.

'We're looking for dry bark and broken twigs,' said one of the little old women.

'But we haven't had any luck,' sighed the second. 'The wood might have been swept clean.'

'Have you been looking long?' asked the little Witch.

'Since this morning,' said the third old woman. 'We've hunted and hunted, but we haven't collected so much as half a basket full. What will become of us if we have so little wood to burn next winter?'

The little Witch glanced at the baskets. They held nothing but a few dry sticks. 'If that's all you've found, I can see why you look sad,' she said to the women. 'Why can't you find anything?'

'It's the wind's fault.'

'The wind?' cried the little Witch. 'How can it be the wind's fault?'

'Because it won't blow,' said the first old woman.

'And if the wind doesn't blow, you see, nothing falls down from the trees.'

'And if no twigs and branches fall down, how are we to fill our baskets?'

'Oh, so that's how it is!' said the little Witch.

The women who were looking for sticks nodded, and one of them said, 'What wouldn't I give to know witchcraft! Then we'd be all right! I'd call up a magic wind. But there, I can't.'

'No, to be sure,' said the little Witch. '*You* can't.'

The three women decided to go home then. 'There's no point in hunting any more,' they said. 'We shan't find anything so long as the wind doesn't blow. Good afternoon!'

'Good afternoon!' said the little Witch. She waited until the three women were a few paces away.

'Couldn't you help them?' Abraxas asked softly.

The little Witch laughed. 'That's just what I'm going to do. Hold tight, or it will blow you away!'

Making a wind was child's play to the little Witch.

She whistled through her teeth – and immediately a whirlwind arose. And what a whirlwind it was! It rushed through the trees, shaking the trunks. It tore the dry twigs off all the trees. Pieces of bark and big branches rattled down on the ground.

The women shrieked and ducked their heads in fright. They held their skirts down with both hands. The whirlwind almost blew them off their feet. But the little Witch didn't let that happen. 'That's enough!' she called. 'Stop!'

The wind obeyed at once. It died away. The wood-gatherers looked timidly round. Then they saw that the wood was full of sticks and broken twigs. 'What luck!' they cried all three. 'So much wood to pick up all at once! It'll last us for weeks!'

They picked up as much as they could carry and stuffed it into their baskets. Then they went home, beaming with joy.

The little Witch watched them go with a smile.

Even Abraxas the raven, for once, was remarkably pleased. 'Not bad for a start!' he said, pecking her shoulder. 'I think you really have the makings of a good witch.'

Forward march

After this the women who came to pick up sticks never had to go home with empty baskets. The little Witch saw to that. They were always cheerful now, and when they met the little Witch they said, smiling happily, 'It's a real pleasure, collecting firewood this year! Coming into the wood is well worth while.'

So the little Witch was very surprised one day when the three women came along the path with tear-stained faces. Their baskets were empty. She had called up a magic wind only yesterday evening, and there must be plenty of sticks and bark.

'Just think what's happened!' sobbed the women. 'The new District Forester has forbidden us to collect sticks! He's emptied the baskets we'd filled – and next time he's going to put us in prison.'

'How friendly of him!' said the little Witch. 'Why's he doing this?'

'Because he's mean!' cried the women. 'The old forester didn't mind at all, it's this new one. You can't think how angry he was. We'll never have cheap firewood again now.'

The women began to cry once more. The little
Witch cheered them up. 'The new forester will think
better of it,' she said. 'I'll bring him to reason.'

'How?' the women wanted to know.'

'Just leave it to me! Go home now and don't worry.
After tomorrow the new forester will let you pick up
as much wood as you can carry.'

The three women went away. Quickly the little
Witch bewitched herself a basket full of firewood. She
put it down at the side of the road and sat down by it,
as if she had been picking up wood and was just
having a little rest. She didn't have to wait long before the new forester came up. She knew him at
once by his green coat, his gun and his leather gamebag.

'Aha!' cried the forester. 'Another one already!
What are you doing there?'

'Resting,' said the little Witch. 'The basket is so
heavy, I must stop for a bit to get my breath back.'

'Don't you know collecting firewood is forbidden?'

'No, how could I know?'

'Well, you know now!' snapped the forester.
'Empty your basket and be off with you.'

'Must I empty my basket?' asked the little Witch.
'Dear Mr Forester, have pity on me! You can't treat a
poor old woman like this!'

'I'll show you how I can treat you!' said the forester

angrily. He seized the basket to empty it. Then the little Witch said,

'You'll leave that alone!'

The forester was furious. 'I'll have you put in prison!' – That was what he meant to shout. But instead he said, 'Please forgive me. I was only joking. Of course you can go on collecting wood.'

'Why on earth did I suddenly say the opposite of what I meant to say?' the startled forester asked himself. He couldn't know that the little Witch had cast a spell on him.

'There now, my son, that sounds better!' she said. 'If only the basket wasn't so heavy!'

'Shall I help you?' asked the forester. 'I could easily carry your firewood home . . .'

She chuckled. 'Really, my boy? How kind you are! What a polite young man!'

'I could hit myself!' thought the new forester. 'What makes me talk such nonsense? I'm not myself at all!' Against his will he had to shoulder the heavy basket.

'If you feel tired, mother, you're welcome to sit on top,' he said.

'Really?' cried the little Witch.

In despair the forester heard himself answer kindly, 'Why, of course! Up you get!'

The little Witch didn't wait for a second invitation. With one bound she swung herself up on top of the full

basket, and the raven hopped on her shoulder.

'Now, off we go! Forward march!'

The forester wished the basket, the old woman and the raven at the bottom of the sea. But wishing didn't help him. He had to trot along like a willing beast of burden.

'Keep straight ahead!' cried Abraxas. 'Gee-up, donkey, faster! Or I'm afraid I shall have to peck your behind.'

The new District Forester went hot and cold by turns. He trotted on and on. Soon he was dripping wet and his tongue was hanging out. He cast off his green hat and then his leather gamebag. He dropped his gun too.

He ran right through the wood like this. 'Left!' Abraxas ordered. 'Right, behind the ditch over there. Then on up the hill!'

When at last they reached the witch's house the forester could hardly stand on his feet. But the little Witch had no pity on him.

'Now, suppose you just chop the firewood up small, my boy?' she asked.

'I'll chop it up, tie it into faggots and put it away,' gasped the forester.

And so he did.

When he had finished – and the work took a long time – the little Witch said,

'You can go home now. Thank you, my son! I'm

sure there's no other forester so kind. How happy the women who come to pick up wood will be! I expect you help everyone like this, don't you?'

The new District Forester staggered away. He dragged himself wearily home to his forester's house. In future he gave a wide berth to any woman collecting wood.

The little Witch had many a good laugh over this trick. 'I'd like to go on doing that,' she told the raven, 'helping good people by punishing bad ones – that's what I enjoy!'

'Is it necessary?' Abraxas replied. 'You could do good in other ways too. Without playing tricks on people, I mean.'

'Oh, that's boring!' she said.

'How do you know?' asked Abraxas.

Paper flowers

One day the little Witch fancied a ride into town. She wanted to have a look at the weekly market there.

Abraxas was delighted. 'Splendid!' he cried. 'I'll come too. It's lonely here at home in the wood, nothing but lots of trees and hardly any people. At market in the town it's just the opposite.'

However, they couldn't very well ride the broomstick right into the market-place; that would have made a great to-do among the people. They would probably have had the police after them too. So they hid the broomstick in a cornfield just outside the town and went in on foot.

In the market-place housewives, maidservants, peasant women and cooks were already crowding round the stalls. Shrill-voiced gardeners' wives were shouting the praises of their vegetables. 'Buy my fine apples and pears!' cried the greengrocers over and over again. The fishwives wanted to sell their salt herrings, the sausage seller wanted to sell his hot frankfurters, the potter had his earthenware jugs and dishes spread out for sale on a pile of straw. Here was

a man shouting, 'Pickled cabbage! Pickled cabbage!'
There was a cry of 'Water melons, pumpkins – much
obliged – water melons, pumpkins!'

The loudest voice of all belonged to Jacob Cheapjack. He stood on the top step to the well in the market-
place, hitting his tray with a hammer and shouting at
the top of his voice,

'Come buy, good people, come buy! Bargains here
today! Prices cut today. I'm giving everything away
half-price! String, snuff, braces! Razor blades, tooth-
brushes, hairclips! Kettle-holders, boot polish, garlic
sauce! Walk up, ladies and gentlemen. Come buy,
come buy! Jacob Cheapjack here!'

The little Witch loved all the noise and bustle. She

let herself drift to and fro
with the crowd. She tasted
the pears here and the
pickled cabbage there. She
spent two pence on a firework from Jacob Cheap-
jack, and he threw in free a
glass ring for her finger.

'Thank you very much,'
said the little Witch.

'Much obliged! – Walk
up, ladies and gentlemen!
Come buy, come buy! Jacob
Cheapjack here!'

Right at the back of the market, in the furthest corner, a pale little girl was standing with a basket of paper flowers, sad and quiet. The people hurried by without noticing her. No one bought anything from the shy little girl.

'Suppose you did a little something for her?' Abraxas suggested. 'I feel very sorry for the poor little child.'

The little Witch made her way through the crowd.

'Can't you sell your flowers?' she asked the little girl.

'Who wants to buy paper flowers in the middle of summer?' said the girl. 'Mother will cry again. If I don't bring any money home in the evening she can't buy us bread. I've got seven brothers and sisters, and Father died last winter. So now we make these paper flowers – but no one ever wants to buy them.'

The little Witch had been listening to the girl sympathetically. For a moment she wondered how to help her. Then she had an idea.

'People don't want to buy your flowers?' she said. 'I can't understand it. They smell so sweet!'

The little girl looked up doubtfully.

'Smell? How could paper flowers have a smell?'

'Indeed they have,' the little Witch assured her earnestly. 'They smell much sweeter than real flowers. Can't you smell them?'

The paper flowers really did smell sweet. The little flower seller was not the only one to notice it.

All over the market-place people began to sniff. 'What's that smell?' they asked each other. 'Impossible! Paper flowers, did you say? Are they for sale? I must get some at once. I wonder if they're very expensive.'

Everyone who had legs and a nose hurried to the corner where the little girl stood. The housewives came running, the servant girls, the peasant women, the cooks, everyone. The fishwives left their salt herrings to look after themselves, the sausage seller left his stove, the gardeners' wives left their vegetables. They all crowded round the girl with the paper flowers, eager to buy. Even Jacob Cheapjack ran up with his tray. He had arrived last of all, so he stood on tiptoe and made a trumpet of his hands. 'Hey, there!' he called over the heads of the crowd. 'Can you hear me, flower-girl? Jacob Cheapjack here! Just hand me a few of those flowers – well, one, at least. Can you hear me? At least one!'

'No going out of turn! Not even for Jacob Cheapjack!' cried the people standing nearest the little girl. 'Sell the flowers in the right order.' 'What a good thing we're in front,' they thought. 'The supply can't hold out long, and all the people who came later will have their trouble for nothing.' – The little girl went on and on selling. But the flowers in her basket never came to an end. There was enough for everyone who wanted to buy, even Jacob Cheapjack.

'The flowers aren't sold out – how's that?' asked the people in surprise, putting their heads together. But the flower-girl herself didn't know. Only the little Witch could have told them. However, she and Abraxas had long since slipped away. They had already left the town houses behind, and soon they would reach the cornfield where the broomstick lay hidden.

The little Witch was still thinking about the flower-girl. She smiled to herself. Then the raven nudged her gently with his beak. He pointed out a black cloud hurrying past overhead. It would not have been suspicious but for a broomstick jutting out of the cloud.

'Look at that!' said Abraxas. 'Aunt Rumpumpel! I suppose the old fright has been spying on you.'

'She spoils everything!' the little Witch grumbled.

'Well, never mind,' said the raven. 'You've nothing to hide from her – least of all what you did today.'

A good lesson

It had rained without stopping for several days. The little Witch had nothing to do but yawn her head off indoors waiting for the weather to clear. Now and then she worked a little magic to pass the time; she made the poker and tongs dance waltzes in the fireplace, she made the dustpan turn somersaults and the butter churn stand on its head. But none of it would do; she soon got bored with it.

When at last the sun was shining outside again, the little Witch couldn't bear to stay in her witch's house any longer. She wanted to be up and doing. 'Come on!' she cried. 'Out through the chimney! I must see if there isn't some magic to be done somewhere.'

'Yes, and good magic in particular,' Abraxas reminded her.

Together they rode over the wood and out into the fields. There were puddles of water everywhere. The paths were muddy: the farm workers were up to their ankles in mud.

The rain had softened the surface of the highroad too. Just then a cart came along from the town. It was

51

drawn by two horses and loaded with beer barrels. On the bad road it could only go slowly. Foam dripped from the horses' mouths as they tugged and strained at the heavy cart. But they weren't going fast enough for the driver. He sat on the box full of self-importance. 'Gee-up!' he shouted. 'Get along, you nags, can't you!' And he lashed them unmercifully with his whip, time and time again.

'It's too bad!' croaked Abraxas indignantly. 'The brute! Thrashing his horses like a hangman! How can anyone stand by and watch?'

'Don't worry,' said the little Witch. 'He'll soon stop.'

They followed the cart until it drew up before the Lion Inn in the next village. The driver unloaded some beer barrels, rolled them across the yard to the cellar, and then went to see the innkeeper in the coffee room and order himself some food. He left the steaming horses harnessed to the cart. They didn't get so much as a handful of hay or oats.

The little Witch waited behind the shed until the driver had disappeared inside the inn. Then she hurried up to the two horses.

'Does he always treat you so badly?' she asked in horse language.

'Yes, always,' said the horses. 'But you should just see him when he's drunk or loses his temper. He even uses the whip handle to beat us then. Look at the marks on our backs. That will show you.'

'The fellow deserves a lesson!' said the little Witch. 'It's a shame the way he treats you! Will you help me pay him out?'

'Certainly – what do you want us to do?'

'When he climbs up ready to drive away, I want you to stay just where you are. Don't move a hoof.'

'You're asking a lot,' replied the horses. 'If we do that he'll beat us black and blue, you wait and see.'

'No harm will come to you,' said the little Witch. 'I promise.'

She went over to the cart and picked up the whip. Then she tied a knot in the end of the whiplash. That was all. Now she could go back behind the shed and lie in wait there with an easy mind, to watch what happened to the driver.

Soon afterwards the driver came out of the inn. He had been eating and drinking. He sauntered up, whistling loud and cheerfully, climbed up to his seat, took the reins in his left hand and with his right hand, by force of habit, reached for the whip. 'Gee-up!' he cried, clicking his tongue, ready to drive away.

When the horses didn't move he grew angry. 'You wait, you lazy brutes!' he shouted. 'I'll give you some help!' And he was just raising his whip to strike –

But his stroke went aside. The blow went nowhere near the horses. The whiplash jerked back and hit the driver's own ears.

'Confound the thing!' he cursed, raising the whip again. He struck a second time – and exactly the same thing happened.

At this, blind rage seized the driver. He jumped up, swinging his whip like a madman to thrash the horses. But every time the blows hit the driver himself. They struck him on his throat, his face, his fingers, on his arms, his trunk and his back.

'Thunder and lightning! This won't do!' he cried at last. He grasped the whip by the other end and struck out furiously with the handle.

He didn't do that a second time.

The whip handle hit him on the nose so hard that blood shot out of his nostrils. The driver cried out aloud. The whip dropped from his hands, everything went dark before his eyes, and he had to prop himself up.

When after a time he came half-way back to his

senses, the little Witch was standing beside the cart. 'If ever you use that whip again, the same thing will happen,' she warned him. 'Get that into your head! You can drive away now, for all I care. Gee-up!'

At her signal the horses went obediently forward. The near horse neighed, 'Thank you very much!' and the off-side horse threw his head up, snorting for joy.

The waggoner sat on his box, a bundle of misery. He swore by his swollen nose, 'I'll never touch a whip again, all my life long!'

Visitors on Friday

Friday is the same for witches as Sunday for other
people. Just as ordinary people are not supposed to
work on Sundays, witches must not cast spells on
Fridays. If they do cast spells in spite of the rule and
get caught they have to pay the penalty.

The little Witch was particularly careful not to
work on Friday. She was determined not to let anything tempt her. On Thursday evening she put
the broomstick away and shut the Book of Witchcraft up in the table drawer – better to be safe
than sorry.

She usually slept late on Friday mornings. Anyway,
if she couldn't cast spells in the morning there wasn't
much else to do. After dinner she generally went for a
little walk, or she sat idle in the shade behind the oven.
'If I had my way,' she often grumbled, 'there'd be
only one Friday every six weeks. And that would be
plenty!'

It was a Friday in late summer. As usual the little
Witch was sitting behind the oven feeling bored. She
would much rather have been casting spells. She

never wanted to cast spells nearly so much any other
day of the week.

All at once she heard footsteps. Then there came a
knock at the door. 'Here I am!' cried the little Witch.
'Just coming!'

She jumped up, full of curiosity, and ran to see who was knocking.

Two children, a boy and a girl, were standing in front of the witch's house holding hands. 'Good afternoon!' they said when they saw the little Witch coming.

'Good afternoon,' said the little Witch. 'What do you want?'

'We're lost,' said the boy, 'so we wanted to ask you the way to the town.'

'We were looking for mushrooms,' the little girl explained.

'Well, well – looking for mushrooms,' repeated the little Witch.

She took the children into the witch's house. There she gave them cocoa, and they each had a piece of her special Friday cake. The little Witch asked their names.

The boy was called Thomas and the girl Veronica. They turned out to be brother and sister. Their parents owned the great inn, The Yoke of Oxen, opposite the well in the market-place.

'I know it,' said the little Witch.

'And what about you?' Thomas asked, looking over the rim of his cup. 'Who are you?'

She chuckled. 'Guess . . .'

'How can I guess? You'll have to tell us.'

'I'm a witch, and this is my witch's house.'

The little girl was frightened. 'Oh!' she cried. 'Are you a real witch – can you cast spells?'

'Don't be afraid,' said the raven soothingly. 'She's a *good* witch. She won't hurt you.'

'No, of course not,' said the little Witch. She poured cocoa out for them both. 'Shall I show you some magic?' she asked.

'Wait a minute!' Abraxas interrupted. 'Have you forgotten it's Friday? Dare you?'

It didn't take the little Witch long to think of a way out. 'We'll just close the shutters,' she said. 'Then no one will see us.'

She closed and bolted the shutters on all the windows. Then she began to cast spells. She made a guinea pig, a hamster and a tortoise appear on the kitchen table. The hamster and the guinea pig got up on their hind legs and danced, but the tortoise didn't want to.

'Come on!' said the little Witch. 'You too.'

So the tortoise had to dance whether he would or no.

'Wonderful!' said Thomas and Veronica. 'How clever you are!'

'That was just a beginning,' said the little Witch. She made the guinea pig, the hamster and the tortoise disappear again, and cast more spells. She worked many other pieces of magic to amuse the children. She made the stove sing a song, and flowers appear in the coffee pot. The wooden whisk and ladle acted a Punch and Judy show on the dresser. The children never grew tired of watching. 'Do some more!' they begged over and over again.

So for two whole hours the little Witch cast one spell after another. Then she said, 'There, that's all. You must go home now.'

'Already?'

'Yes, and high time too. You want to be home before dark, don't you?'

For the first time the children realized that it was getting late. They picked up their mushroom baskets.

'Oh!' said Thomas in surprise. 'But we'd hardly found any – and now our baskets are full of mushrooms!'

'Fancy that,' said the little Witch, pretending to be surprised too.

Quickly she set the children on their way.

'Thank you very much!' said Veronica as they parted. 'Suppose you came to see us one day? We'll take you all over the inn, and show you the kitchen and the cellar, and Corbinian the ox in his stall.'

'Who's he?' asked Abraxas.

'He's our pet,' said Thomas. 'We can ride on his back! Will you come, then?'

'We'll come,' said the little Witch. 'When would it suit you?'

'Two weeks on Sunday,' Thomas decided. 'That's the day of the shooting match. We'll meet on the shooting ground.'

'Right,' said the little Witch. 'We'll come two weeks on Sunday, then. Run along now!'

Thomas and Veronica held hands and ran off towards the town. The little Witch turned home. 'I wish all Fridays went so fast!' she thought.

When she got home, there was a pitch-black cloud hovering over the roof of the witch's house.

'You've done it now!' croaked Abraxas. 'Rumpumpel the storm-witch was watching. Down the chimney, I suppose.'

'It might just be an ordinary black cloud,' suggested the little Witch in confusion. 'I can't see a broomstick, at any rate . . .'

But secretly she was very worried. Suppose it really was Aunt Rumpumpel? What bad luck! She would complain to the Head Witch at once that the little Witch had been casting spells on a Friday.

'Let's wait and see what happens,' she said meekly.

She waited for a whole week, day by day. But nothing happened. She wasn't summoned before the Head Witch for punishment.

'So it wasn't Aunt Rumpumpel after all, then,' thought the little Witch in relief.

The bewitched shooting match

The bells were ringing, the cannon were booming, and there was hardly room for all the happy people in the meadow outside the town. The little Witch was looking out for Thomas and Veronica. She thrust her way through the crowd. Abraxas the raven almost put his neck out of joint.

Where could the two children be hiding?

Thomas and Veronica were sitting behind the marquee. They were in the depths of despair. After a long search the little Witch found them.

'Well, what long faces!' she cried, shaking her head. 'How can anyone look so miserable on the Sunday of the shooting match?'

'We can,' said Thomas. 'Father has offered our ox as the prize.'

'Corbinian the ox?' asked the little Witch.

'Yes,' sobbed Veronica. 'He's the prize for the champion shot.'

'And the winner will have him killed and roasted,' Thomas told the little Witch, 'and then all the marksmen will eat him up.'

'But suppose no one wins the ox?' the little Witch suggested. 'That might happen . . .'

'No, it couldn't happen,' replied Thomas. 'You can't have a shooting match without a champion shot.'

'Plenty of things can happen,' said the little Witch. She had already decided on a plan. 'You come with me. Everything will be all right.'

Hesitating, the two children followed the little Witch back to the shooting ground. The marksmen were just arriving. In front marched the Captain with a drawn sword; at the back trotted Corbinian the ox, with ribbons and bright streamers draped all over him.

'Hurrah!' cried all the people, craning their necks.

They all wanted to watch the shooting match and see who won the ox.

'Company – halt!' ordered the Captain. Then he made the band sound a flourish on their trumpets.

'Hush! The Captain's going to make a speech!' hissed the crowd.

'May I bid you all a hearty welcome to our shooting match,' said the Captain. 'Today our special thanks are due to the generous owner of the inn, The Yoke of

Oxen, who has given a live ox for the prize of victory.'

'Hurrah!' shouted all the people once more. 'Long live the host of the Oxen! Long live our noble benefactor!'

'And now I declare our shooting match open!' said the Captain of the marksmen, waving his sword.

At one end of the meadow stood a tall post. A wooden eagle was fastened to the top. The marksmen had to shoot it down.

Naturally the Captain had the first shot – and his shot went quite wide.

'These things happen,' said the crowd.

The Captain stepped back, feeling ashamed of himself.

The Lieutenant was the next to try his luck. He took aim and fired – but again the shot went wide.

The crowd began to smile. Soon they were laughing. They could understand one shot fired by one man missing the eagle. But when all the shots fired by all the marksmen missed, they split their sides laughing. Had anyone ever seen the like of it?

'Incredible!' muttered the Captain chewing in a puzzled way at his moustache. He was so ashamed, he wished the ground would open and swallow him up. He had no idea that the little Witch had bewitched his rifle, and the rifles of all the other marksmen.

But the children from the Oxen knew what was

going on. At every shot that went wide they grew happier. 'Wonderful!' they cried. 'Splendid!'

When the last marksman had shot, the little Witch nudged Thomas. 'You go forward now,' she said.

'What am I to do?'

'Have a shot!'

The boy understood. He made his way to the open space in front of the post.

'You, you imp?' cried the Captain. He was going to send him back again. But at that the people shouted, 'No, let him have a shot! We want him to have a shot!' They thought that would be funniest of all.

'All right,' said the Captain angrily. 'But he won't have much luck.'

Thomas picked up a rifle. He levelled it and took aim like a veteran.

The people held their breath. They stood on tiptoe, watching the eagle in suspense.

There was a flash and a bang. The eagle toppled off the post. Thomas was the champion shot!

'Hurrah!' cried all the people, waving their hats in the air. 'Long live Thomas! Thomas from the Oxen has won the ox.'

They stormed the shooting ground and raised the happy marksman on their shoulders.

'Up on the ox with him! Up on the ox!'

'Me too!' cried Veronica.

'Come on up,' said Thomas. 'It's your ox too.'

If the two children had had their way, the little Witch would have been hoisted up on the back of Corbinian the ox as well. But she refused to come. Thomas and Veronica had to ride into town on the ox by themselves.

Before them went the band playing one joyful march after another. Behind followed the Captain and his men with sour faces. The crowd waved wildly. 'Bravo!' they shouted. 'Long live the champion!'

On the way a gentleman from the newspaper thrust his way up to the children. 'And when is the ox to be roasted?' he asked, opening his notebook and sucking his pencil.

'The ox isn't going to be roasted at all,' replied Thomas. 'He's going back to his stall, and there he'll stay.'

The bells rang, the cannon boomed. No one noticed the little Witch climb on her broomstick behind the marquee and ride happily away.

'You've brought it off again!' Abraxas praised her. 'If you ask me, that cancels out the spells you cast on a Friday.'

The chestnut man

Winter had come. A snowstorm howled round the witch's house, beating on the shutters. The little Witch didn't mind. She sat on the bench in front of the tiled stove then, day in, day out, warming her back. On her feet she wore thick felt slippers. From time to time she clapped her hands. Whenever she clapped, one of the logs lying in the box by the grate leapt into the opening of the stove of its own accord. And if she happened to fancy a baked apple, she had only to snap her fingers. At once apples came rolling along from the larder and hopped into the hearth.

Abraxas the raven was very happy. 'This really is a splendid way to spend the long winter!' he kept saying.

But in time the little Witch grew tired of her lazy life. 'Am I to sit on the bench by the stove warming my back all winter?' she said peevishly one day. 'I need fresh air and exercise again. Come on, let's go out for a ride.'

'What?' cried Abraxas in horror. 'Do you take me

for a penguin? This freezing cold is no weather for me,
thank you very much for the invitation! Let's stay at
home in the warm!'

'Just as you like,' said the little Witch. 'You can stay at home, for all I care. I shall just go out riding by myself. I'm not afraid of the cold. I shall wrap up warm enough.'

The little Witch put on seven petticoats, one on top of the other. Then she tied her big woollen kerchief round her head, got into her winter boots and put two pairs of mittens on. Wrapped up like this she jumped on her broomstick and flew out up the chimney.

It was bitterly cold outside. The trees wore thick white coats. The moss and stones had disappeared under the snow. Here and there, footprints and sleigh tracks led through the wood.

The little Witch steered her broomstick towards the nearest village. The farmyards were snowed right under, and the church tower wore a fluffy snow cap. Smoke climbed from all the chimneys. As she rode by, the little Witch heard the farmers and their men threshing corn in the barns – thump-thump-thump, thump-thump-thump.

There were swarms of children tobogganing on the hills behind the village. People were skiing too. The little Witch watched them race downhill. Soon afterwards a truck came along to sand the road. She followed that for a little while, and then she joined a flock of crows flying towards the town.

'I'll go into the town and have a walk, to warm myself up a bit,' she thought. For by now she was

miserably cold, in spite of her seven petticoats and two pairs of mittens.

There was no need to hide the broomstick this time; she carried it over her shoulder. Now she looked just like an ordinary little old woman going to sweep the snow away. No one who met her thought anything of it. All the people were in a hurry and trudged past her with bent heads.

The little Witch would have been only too pleased to have another look at the displays in the shop windows. But the panes were all frosted over with flowers of ice. The well in the market-place was frozen, and icicles hung from the inn signs.

In the market-place there was a narrow wooden stall painted green. There was an iron stove in front of it, and behind the stove, with his back to the stall, stood a shrivelled little man. He wore a big driving coat and felt shoes. He had turned up his collar and pulled his cap down over his forehead. From time to time the little man sneezed. Whenever he sneezed the spray fell hissing on the glowing top of the stove.

'What are you doing there?' the little Witch asked the man.

'Can't you see? I'm – a-tishoo! – I'm roasting Spanish chestnuts.'

'Spanish chestnuts? What do you mean?'

'Sweet chestnuts,' the little man explained. 'Would you like to try some?' he asked, taking the lid off the stove. 'A penny the small bag, two pence the big one. A-tishoo!'

The smell of roast chestnuts rose to the little Witch's nostrils. 'I'd love to taste them,' she said, 'but I haven't any money with me.'

'Never mind, then, I'll give you a few for nothing,' said the little man. 'You can do with something warm in this wicked cold. A-tishoo! and that's the truth.'

The little man blew his nose. Then he took a hand-

ful of chestnuts out of the stove and put them in a
brown paper bag. He gave it to the little Witch.

'There you are!' he said. 'But you must shell them
before you put them in your mouth.'

'Thank you very much,' said the little Witch. She
tried the chestnuts. 'Mm, how good they are!' she
cried in surprise. Then she said,

'You know, one could almost envy you! You have
easy work, and standing by the warm stove you
needn't be cold.'

'Don't say that!' the little man contradicted her.
'Standing about in the cold all day, you get frozen just
the same. Even the iron stove doesn't help. At most
you burn your fingers on it getting the hot chestnuts
out. A-tishoo! But apart from that, let me tell you, my
feet are a pair of icicles. And as for my nose – isn't it as
red as a candle on a Christmas tree? I shall never get
rid of this cold. It's dreadful.'

As if to prove it, the little man sneezed again. It was
such a heart-rending sneeze that the wooden stall
rocked and the market-place echoed.

I can help him, the little Witch thought. Wait a
minute . . . And she murmured a magic spell to herself.

'Are your toes still cold?' she asked.

'Not just at the moment,' said the man. 'I think the
cold has eased off a little. I can tell by the end of my
nose. I wonder how that happened?'

'Don't ask me,' said the little Witch. 'I must ride home now.'

'*Ride* home!'

'Did I say ride? You must have heard wrong.'

'Perhaps I did,' said the little man. 'Good day.'

'Good day,' said the little Witch. 'And thank you very much!'

'Not at all – don't mention it.'

Soon afterwards two boys came running across the market-place. 'Quick, quick, Mr Chestnut man!' they cried. 'A penny-worth for each of us!'

'Two penny-worths, certainly. Much obliged!'

The chestnut man reached into the stove.

But for the first time in all his long career as a chestnut man he didn't burn his fingers on the hot chestnuts. He never burnt them again at all. His toes never froze again, either, and no more did his nose. His cold was gone for good; it might have been blown away. And if ever he wanted to sneeze again, the good chestnut man had to take a pinch of snuff.

Better than seven petticoats

The little Witch reached home again towards dusk. Abraxas the raven at once wanted to hear what had happened on her ride.

'I'll t-tell you later,' answered the little Witch, her teeth chattering. 'First I must m-make t-tea. I'm so c-cold, I c-can hardly s-speak.'

'There you are!' croaked Abraxas. 'That's because you simply *would* go out riding in this dreadful cold! But you just wouldn't listen to me.'

The little Witch made herself a big pot of herb tea. She sweetened it with plenty of sugar. Then she sipped the hot brew. It did her good, and soon she grew warmer again. Then she took off her seven petticoats, down to the bottom one, stripped off her shoes and stockings and got into her slippers.

'I won't deny it, I did get frozen stiff,' she said. 'But it was fun all the same, let me tell you.'

She sat down on the bench by the stove and began to tell her story. Abraxas the raven listened to her in silence. Not till the story of the chestnut man was told did he interrupt her to say,

'You know, I just don't understand at all. You help
this chestnut man to keep warm by witchcraft, but
you didn't help yourself! What's a reasonable bird
supposed to make of that?'

'What do you mean?' asked the little Witch.

'What do you think I mean? If I were you and I
could work magic, *I* wouldn't need herb tea to warm
me up, certainly not! I wouldn't let things get to that
pass.'

'But I did all I could!' said the little Witch. 'I put on
two pairs of mittens, and my winter boots, and my
woollen kerchief, and seven petticoats.'

'Bah!' said Abraxas. 'I'd know a better way to keep
the cold off than seven petticoats.'

'Better than seven petticoats?'

'Much better. As sure as I'm a raven and my name's Abraxas.'

The little Witch still didn't understand. 'Tell me what you think I should have done,' she asked him. 'But you must be clearer and not keep talking in riddles.'

'Talking in riddles, am I?' said Abraxas. 'It's as clear as day. If you can cast spells to keep the chestnut man from freezing, why, may I ask, why can't you cast the same spells for yourself?'

'Goodness me!' cried the little Witch, clapping her hand to her forehead. 'That's perfectly true! Why on earth didn't I think of that before? You're quite right -- after all, what's the use of being a witch?'

'Exactly,' Abraxas agreed. 'Sometimes you seem to forget you're a witch at all. It's a good thing you've got someone to remind you now and then.'

The little Witch nodded eagerly in reply.

'Yes,' she said, 'you really are the wisest raven that ever hatched out of an egg. Of course – I'll follow your advice on the spot. And if you like I'll betwitch you with my spell to keep the cold off too, so you won't have to stay at home in the future when I go out riding.'

'All right,' said Abraxas. 'I don't mind having you do *me* a good turn for once.'

So the little Witch cast a spell to keep herself and

the raven from getting frozen again. After that they could go out for rides, even in the bitterest weather, without feeling the cold at all. They didn't have to wrap up specially warm, and they didn't need herb tea afterwards.

And although they went out almost every day after this, they never caught colds again.

Snowman

It was a beautiful, sunny winter's day. The sky shone bright blue and the snow gleamed pure white as a newly washed linen handkerchief. The little Witch was sitting at the edge of the wood with Abraxas the raven, sunning herself. All at once they heard children's voices shouting happily somewhere near. The little Witch sent Abraxas the raven off to see what was going on. After a little while he came back.

'It's some children,' he said, 'tiny little scraps about six or seven years old. They're building themselves a snowman over there in the meadow behind the hedge.

'I must have a look at it,' said the little Witch. It wasn't far to the meadow behind the hedge, so she went on foot.

The snowman was just finished. He had a carrot stuck in his face for a nose and lumps of coal for eyes. His hat was a battered old saucepan. He held a birch broom proudly in his right hand.

The children didn't notice the little Witch when she appeared from behind the hedge. They were holding

hands and dancing round the snowman, hopping from one leg to the other. As they danced they sang.

> *Snowman with your nose so red,*
> *Old tin saucepan on your head,*
> *Snowman with your coat so white,*
> *Don't you think the frost will bite?*

The little Witch was delighted with the beautiful snowman and the children. She would have liked to join in and dance with them.

But then, all of a sudden, some big boys came running out of the wood nearby, seven of them in all. Shouting and yelling, they fell on the snowman and threw him to the ground. They kicked the saucepan about and broke the broomstick in two, and they rubbed snow in the faces of the children who had just been dancing so happily. Goodness knows what else they might have done to the children if the little Witch hadn't stepped in.

'Hi there!' she said angrily to the big boys. 'You leave the children alone. If you don't stop it I'll give you a good thrashing with my broomstick!'

At that the big boys ran away. But the lovely snowman was spoilt. The children felt very sad and hung their heads. The little Witch understood. She tried to comfort the children.

'Build yourselves a new snowman,' she suggested. 'What about that?'

'If we build another snowman the big boys will come and throw the new one over too,' said the children. 'Besides, they've broken our broom in two, and we haven't got another.'

'I think it only *seemed* broken,' said the little Witch, bending over the broken broom. 'There – look at it.'

_ She showed the broom to the children. They saw that it was mended.

'Build your snowman and don't worry,' the little

Witch encouraged the children. 'You needn't be afraid of the big boys. If they come back they'll get what they deserve, you can be sure of that!'

The children let her persuade them. They built a new snowman. He was even finer and more magnificent than the first one, because the little Witch was lending a hand this time.

But when the new snowman was finished, it wasn't long before the seven boys came tearing out of the wood again shouting and yelling. The children were frightened and wanted to run away.

'Stay here!' cried the little Witch. 'See what's going to happen.'

And what did happen when the seven boys came charging up?

Suddenly the new snowman began to move. Swinging his birch broom like a club he defended himself against the big boys.

He struck the first one on his fur cap with the broomstick. He gave the second a good smack on the nose with his left hand. He caught hold of the third and the fourth and knocked their heads together so hard that you could hear the crack. He flung the fifth against the sixth, so that they both fell flat on the ground taking the seventh along with them.

Once they were all lying there the snowman took his broom and swept up a big heap of snow over the boys.

That was more than they had bargained for.

They tried to shout for help, but they only swallowed snow. They threshed about desperately with their arms and legs. When at last, and with great difficulty, they had struggled free, they ran away in terror.

The snowman went calmly back to his place and stiffened up again. He stood there as if nothing at all had happened.

The children shouted for joy, for the big boys would never come back again, that was certain. And the little Witch laughed so loud over the success of her trick the tears came into her eyes, and Abraxas the raven cried in alarm,

'Stop, stop, or you'll burst!'

What do you bet?

How did there come to be two little Negro boys in the snow-covered village street? And since when had there been Turks and Indians in these parts? Turks with red caps and wide baggy trousers – and Indians with faces painted fiercely, waving long spears over their heads.

'They must be from the circus,' thought Abraxas the raven.

But the two little Negro boys didn't come from the circus. No more did the Turks and Indians. The Chinese women, the cannibal, the Eskimo girls, the desert sheikh and the Hottentot chief were not part of the show either. No – it was carnival time in the village. The children had a half-holiday from school because of the carnival, and they were romping about the village square in fancy dress.

The little Turks threw paper streamers. 'Wah! Waah!' roared the Hottentot chief. 'I'm hungry!' shouted the cannibal. 'Who wants to be gobbled up? I'm hungrrry!' The Chinese girls talking in Chinese, the Eskimo women chattered in Eskimo language, and the cowboys shot corks into the air from the pistols. The chimney sweep flourished his cardboard top hat, Punch hit the desert sheikh on the turban with his wooden sword, and Jaromir the robber chief made such dreadful faces that his moustache came unstuck and kept falling off.

'Do you see the little witch over there.' asked Abraxas after a while.

'Where?'

'Over by the fire station. With the long broom!'

'Oh yes – I see her,' said the little Witch. 'But I must go and have a closer look.'

She ran up to the carnival witch and said, 'Good afternoon!'

'Hullo,' said the carnival witch. 'Are you my sister by any chance?'

'Perhaps,' said the real little Witch. 'How old are you?'

'Twelve. How old are you?'

'A hundred and twenty-seven and a half.'

'What fun!' cried the carnival witch. 'I must remember that! From now on, when the others ask how old I am, I'll say two hundred and fifty-nine and three-quarters!'

'But it's my real age!'

'Yes, of course it's your real age. And you can really cast spells and ride on a broomstick too!'

'Of course I can!' cried the real little Witch. 'What do you bet me?'

'Let's not bet anything,' said the carnival witch. 'After all, you can't really.'

'What do you bet me?' repeated the real little Witch.

The carnival witch burst out laughing. 'Come here, you Chinese girls!' she shouted. 'And the Turks and the Negro boys, you come here too. All of you – the desert sheikh and the Eskimos and the cannibal.

Here's a little witch who can ride on a broomstick!'

'She can't possibly,' said Punch.

'Yes, yes!' cried the carnival witch. 'She wanted to have a bet with me. Now let's see if she was telling the truth.'

In a trice all the children had surrounded the two witches. The chimney sweep, Jaromir the robber chief, Punch and the Indians, the Hottentot chief, the Turks and the little Negro boys, they all came crowding up, laughing and shouting.

'Don't try and trick us,' cried the Eskimo girls.

'Or we'll tie you to the stake!' threatened the Indian, Red Cloud.

'If you've tricked us,' roared the cannibal, 'I shall gobble you up for a punishment! Do you hear? And let me tell you, I'm hungrrry!'

'Gobble me up and welcome, if you're hungry,' said the little Witch. 'But you'd better look sharp, or I shall be off!'

The cannibal was going to grab the little Witch by the collar But the little Witch moved faster. She jumped on her broomstick – and whoosh! she was up in the air.

The cannibal flopped down on his behind in fright. The Negro boys and the Turks, the Chinese girls and the Eskimos, they all fell silent. The desert sheikh's turban fell off. The robber chief forgot to make faces. Red Cloud, the bold Indian brave, went pale under his war paint. The little Negro boys turned as white as chalk, but luckily no one could see because they had blacked their faces with soot.

The little Witch rode round the village square laughing. Then she settled on the roof of the fire station and waved down. Abraxas the raven perched on her shoulder and croaked,

'Hi, you down there! Now do you believe she can cast spells?'

'But I can do lots more magic!' said the little Witch, 'The cannibal was so hungry . . .'

She spread out her fingers and murmured something. Then a shower of carnival pancakes and fritters pattered down into the village square! Shouting for joy, all the children fell on the rich dainties and ate as much as they wanted. Even the cannibal didn't despise the pancakes, though they were not really his usual diet.

Only the carnival witch ate nothing. She looked after the real little Witch, who was riding away on her broomstick now, chuckling.

'Well, fancy that!' thought the carnival witch. 'Perhaps she really is a hundred and twenty-seven and a half after all.'

Carnival in the wood

'A carnival,' remarked Abraxas the raven that evening, when they were sitting in the warm at home waiting for the baked apples to be done, 'a carnival is a splendid thing! What a pity there's no carnival here in the wood.'

'Carnival in the wood?' asked the little Witch, looking up from the stocking she was knitting. 'Why shouldn't we have a carnival here in the wood?'

'I don't know,' said the raven. 'But that's how it is, and there's no changing it.'

The little Witch smiled to herself. The raven's words had given her an amusing idea. But she said nothing about it yet. She got up, went to the stove and took out the baked apples. When they had eaten the apples she said,

'I've got a kindness to ask of you, dear Abraxas. Fly through the wood tomorrow morning and tell the animals you meet to come to the witch's house in the afternoon.'

'I can do that all right,' said Abraxas. 'Only the

94

animals will want to know *why* you're inviting them. What do I say then?'

'Tell them,' said the little Witch in a careless voice, 'tell them I'm asking them to a carnival.'

'What?' cried Abraxas, as if he couldn't have heard right. 'A carnival, did you say?'

'Yes. I'm asking them to a carnival,' repeated the little Witch. 'A carnival in the wood.'

At this Abraxas the raven bombarded the little Witch with a thousand questions. What was her plan? he wanted to know. And would there be Negro boys and Chinese and Eskimos at this carnival too?

'Wait and see!' said the little Witch. 'If I told you all about it today you wouldn't enjoy it half so much tomorrow.'

They left it at that.

So next day Abraxas the raven flew through the wood telling the animals they were all to come to the witch's house that afternoon. And if they met other animals they were to pass the message on. The more who came to the carnival the merrier, he told them.

And so that afternoon they came streaming along from all directions – squirrels, deer and hares, two stags, a dozen rabbits and troops of field mice. The little Witch welcomed them. When they had all arrived she said,

'Now we'll have the carnival.'

'How do you do that?' squeaked the field mice.

'Everyone must be different from usual today,' the
little Witch explained. 'You can't dress up as Chinese
or Turks, of course, but I can do magic instead.'

She had already decided what the magic should be.

She cast spells to give the hare's stag's antlers, and
the stags hare's ears. She made the field mice grow
until they were as big as rabbits, and she made the
rabbits shrink until they were as small as field mice.

She gave the deer red and green fur and made raven's wings for the squirrels.

'What about me?' cried Abraxas. 'You're not forgeting me, are you?'

'Of course not,' said the little Witch. 'You shall have a squirrel's tail.'

She gave herself owl's eyes and horse's teeth. They made her look almost as ugly as Aunt Rumpumpel.

When they were all disguised it should have been time for the carnival to start. But suddenly they heard a hoarse voice over by the oven.

'Might one join the party?' asked the voice, and when the animals looked round, mystified, a fox came slinking round the oven.

'I wasn't invited, I know,' said the fox, 'but I'm sure the ladies and gentlemen won't mind me making so bold as to come to the carnival all the same . . .'

The hares shook their stag's antlers in fright, the squirrels prudently fluttered up on the witch's house, and the field mice got behind the little Witch for safety.

'Send him away!' cried the terrified rabbits. 'This is too much! We're never safe from this rascal in the ordinary way. Now that we're the size of field mice he's more dangerous than ever.'

The fox looked hurt. 'Perhaps I'm not fine enough for the ladies and gentlemen?' Wagging his tail, he begged the little Witch, 'Do let me join in!'

'If you promise not to hurt anyone . . .'

'I promise,' he said in honeyed tones. 'I give you my word. If I break my promise, may I eat nothing but potatoes and carrots all my life!'

'That would be hard on you,' said the little Witch. 'But I hope it won't come to that.' She didn't trust the fox's fair words, so she settled the matter by casting a spell which gave him a duck's bill.

Now the other animals could be happy, for with the best will in the world the fox couldn't possibly eat them. Even the tiny shrunken rabbits had no need to fear him.

The carnival in the wood lasted until late in the evening. The squirrels played Catch, Abraxas the raven teased the red and green deer with his bushy tail, the rabbits hopped about in front of the fox's bill, and the field mice got up on their hind legs and

squeaked at the stags. 'Don't you be conceited – you're not much bigger than us!' The stags bore them no grudge; they pricked up their hare's ears, first the right ear, then the left, and besides, they thought, a carnival is a carnival.

'It's nearly time to stop,' said the little Witch at last, when the moon had risen. 'But you must have something to eat before you go home.'

She bewitched a load of hay for the deer and the

stags, a basket of hazelnuts for the squirrels, and oats and beechnuts for the field mice. She gave the rabbits and hares half a head of cabbage each. But first she changed all the animals back to their ordinary size and shape and shade. All but the fox.

'Excuse me, please!' quacked the fox with his duck's bill. 'Can't I have my snout back too? And if you're giving the deer and hares something to eat, what about me?'

'Be patient,' said the little Witch. 'You're not going to lose by it. Just wait till the other guests have said good night. Till then – well, you know what to do.'

The fox had to wait till the last field mouse was

safely back in its hole. Only then did the little Witch rid the fox of his duck's bill. He bared his teeth in relief and set ravenously about the smoked sausage that he suddenly found lying in the snow under his nose.

'Does it taste good?' asked the little Witch.

But the fox was so busy with his sausage that he made no answer – and that, after all, was answer enough.

A game of skittles

The sun had chased winter away. The ice had thawed and the snow was melted. Spring flowers were already blooming in every nook and cranny. The willows had decked themselves out with beautiful silver catkins, and buds were swelling on the birch trees and hazel bushes.

No wonder all the people that the little Witch met these days looked happy. They were glad of the spring. 'Thank goodness winter's over at last,' they thought. 'We've had to put up with it quite long enough.'

One day the little Witch was going for a walk in the fields. At the edge of one field sat a woman. She looked so miserable that it went to the little Witch's heart.

'What's the matter?' she asked kindly. 'That's no way to look in this lovely weather! Spring has come, haven't you noticed?'

'Spring?' said the woman sadly. 'Well, you may be right, but what's the good of that? Spring or winter, it's all the same to me. The same cares, the same

sorrows. I wish I were dead and buried in the ground.'

'Come, come!' cried the little Witch. 'You shouldn't be talking of dying at your age. You'd better tell me what's worrying you, and then we'll see if I can help.'

'You couldn't possibly help me,' sighed the woman. 'But I'll tell you my story, all the same. It's my husband. He's a tile-maker. You don't earn a fortune making tiles, but what the tile-making brings in would be enough to keep us from starving. If only my husband didn't waste all his money in the skittle alley! Night after night, he throws away the money he earned in the daytime playing skittles with his friends in the tavern. There's nothing left over for me and the children. Can you blame me for wishing I were dead and buried?'

'But haven't you ever tried to make your husband see reason?' asked the little Witch.

'I've tried and tried!' said the woman. 'It would be easier to melt a stone. He won't listen to me – nothing I say does any good.'

'If talking to him doesn't help, we must get at him some other way!' said the little Witch. 'Tomorrow morning bring me some hairs from your husband's head. Quite a small tuft will do. Then we'll see.'

The tile-maker's wife did as the little Witch told her. Early next morning she came to the edge of the field bringing a tuft of her husband's hair with her. She gave it to the little Witch, saying,

'I cut this tuft of hair off his head last night while he was asleep. Here you are. But I don't see how it can help you.'

'It's to help you, not me,' said the little Witch mysteriously. 'Go home now, and just wait and see what happens. Your husband will lose all his taste for skittles. He'll be cured before the week is out!'

The woman went home. She could see no sense in it. But the little Witch knew exactly what she was doing. She buried the tile-maker's hair at the nearest crossroads, repeating all kinds of magic spells over it. Finally she scratched a magic sign in the sand with her fingernail, on the exact spot where the hairs were buried. Then she winked at Abraxas the raven.

'There!' she said. 'The tile-maker had better be ready for a shock!'

That evening the tile-maker went to play skittles as usual. He drank his beer with the other players. Then he asked, 'Shall we start?'

'Yes, let's start!' they all cried.

'Who's to have first go?'

'Anyone who likes!' it was decided.

'Good,' said the tile-maker, reaching for the ball. 'Then I'll knock all nine skittles down at once. Just watch them tumble over!'

He gave a mighty swing of his arm. Then he rolled the ball.

The ball rolled thumpety-thump along the skittle alley. It crashed into the skittles with a thunderous noise, and crack! off flew the king skittle's head! The ball rolled on and struck the wall with a loud crash, making a big hole in it.

'Hey, you – tile-maker!' cried the skittle players. 'What's the idea? Do you want to break up the skittle alley?'

'That's funny,' muttered the tile-maker. 'Must have been something to do with the ball. I'll use another next time.'

But his next turn, when it came round again, was even more disastrous, although he had chosen the smallest ball of all. It shattered two skittles to pieces, so that the chips whirred round the scorer's ears – and it made another hole in the wall.

'Look here!' the other players threatened the tile-maker. 'Either you roll the ball a bit more gently in future, or we shan't let you play skittles with us any more.'

'I'll be very careful,' the tile-maker promised them faithfully.

He rolled the ball for the third time. It was the most cautious, gentle shot he had ever made in his life. He pushed the ball off with only two fingers – but crash! it rolled through the middle of the skittles and struck the corner post with such force that it broke in half.

The post heeled over and half the ceiling crashed down. Planks and pieces of beams fell like hail; laths, bits of plaster and roof tiles rattled to the ground. It was like an earthquake.

The skittle players stared at one another, pale with fright. But when they had got over the first shock, they took their beer mugs and flung them at the tile-maker.

'You be off!' they shouted furiously. 'Get out! We

don't want anything to do with a man who breaks the skittle alley to pieces. Play skittles anywhere you like in future – but you won't play here!'

On the following evenings, at the other skittle alleys in the village and the surrounding villages, just the same thing happened to the tile-maker. It never took more than three shots to bring the ceiling tumbling down. Then the other players threw beer mugs at the tile-maker and wished he were in the moon. Before the week was out there was nowhere left for him to play skittles. 'For goodness' sake!' people cried wherever he appeared. 'It's the tile-maker! Quick, hide the skittles and put the balls away. Don't let that man get his hands on them, or something dreadful will happen!'

In the end the tile-maker had no choice but to give up skittles for good. Instead of going out to the tavern every evening he always stayed at home now. He found that dull at first, to be sure, but in time he got used to it, for the little Witch's magic spells had taken care of that too.

After this the woman and her children were in no danger of starving, and the little Witch could be happy to think how she had helped them.

Stuck fast

Abraxas the raven was a confirmed bachelor. 'Life is far more comfortable for a bachelor,' he used to say. 'In the first place you needn't build a nest. In the second place you needn't be bothered with a wife. And in the third place, you're spared having to look after half a dozen hungry chicks year after year. They eat you out of house and home first, and then they fly away in any case. I've heard about it from my brothers and sisters. They're all old married people, and I wouldn't change places with any of them.'

Abraxas the raven's closest brother was called Krax. His nest was in the tall elm tree on the bank of the duckpond in the nearby village. Abraxas paid him a visit once a year, in the time between Easter and Whit Sunday. By then, of course, his sister-in-law had laid the new eggs, but she had not hatched them out yet. So Abraxas ran no risk of having to help his brother and sister-in-law feed their greedy chicks.

This time when Abraxas came back from his visit to Krax and his wife the little Witch could see that something was wrong from a mile off.

'Has anything happened to your brother Krax?'
she asked him.

'Not yet, I'm glad to say,' Abraxas answered. 'But
my brother and his wife are in great trouble. There
are two boys who have been strolling near his home for
several days past, climbing all the trees and stealing
the nests. The day before yesterday they robbed a
blackbird's nest, yesterday a nest belonging to
magpies. They pocketed the eggs and threw the nests
in the duckpond. My brother Krax is in despair. If
things go on like this, the boys will get to his nest
sooner or later.'

'Your brother Krax need not worry,' said the little
Witch. 'Fly back and give him my kind regards. Tell
him to hurry here and let me know if the boys climb

the elm to get at his nest. I'll get rid of these scamps for him!'

'Will you really?' cried Abraxas. 'You are a good witch, anyone can see that! The Head Witch will be pleased with you! I'll fly and tell Krax and his wife at once.'

Several days passed and nothing happened. The little Witch forgot all about the two nest robbers. But one afternoon towards the end of the week brother Krax came flying breathlessly up.

'They've come, they've come!' he began croaking even before he arrived. 'Come quickly, little Witch, before it's too late!'

The little Witch had just been grinding coffee, but she put the coffee mill down on the kitchen table at once, ran for her broomstick and flew like the wind to the duckpond. The brothers Krax and Abraxas could hardly keep up with her, she flew over the wood so fast.

By this time the two boys were high up on the old elm tree. They could almost reach the raven's nest. Mrs Krax was crouching over her eggs, trembling.

'Hi there, you two!' cried the little Witch. 'What are you doing there? Come down!'

The two boys were frightened. But when they saw it was only a little old woman calling up to them, one of them put his tongue out at the little Witch and the other made a face at her.

'Come down, I tell you!' the little Witch warned them. 'Or you'll catch it!'

But the two boys just laughed at her. 'Come and get us, if you can!' one of them answered rudely. 'We'll stay sitting up here as long as we like. Yah!'

'Very well!' said the little Witch. 'You can stay up there and welcome!'

And she cast a spell to make the two nest robbers stick fast. They could climb neither up nor down. They stayed clinging just where they were, as if rooted to the spot.

Now Abraxas and Krax and Mrs Krax attacked the boys with their beaks and claws. They nipped and pecked and scratched them until they were sore all over. The egg robbers began to cry out in despair. Their cries for help were so loud and miserable that half the village heard the noise and came running to the duckpond.

'What's going on, for heaven's sake?' asked the people in alarm. 'Why, just look, it's Fritz the tailor's son and Sepp the cobbler's son! Were they going to rob the raven's nest, I wonder? Well, it serves them right. They've got what they deserve. What do they have to go climbing trees and stealing eggs for?'

No one felt sorry for them. The only odd thing, so people thought, was that Fritz and Sepp didn't make their escape. Even when the ravens at last left them alone they stayed perched up on the tree.

'Come down, you two heroes!' called the villagers.

'We can't!' wailed Fritz the tailor's son, and Sepp the cobbler's son sobbed, 'Boo-hoo, we're stuck! We can't get down.'

In the end the fire brigade had to turn out. The firemen put tall ladders up and brought down the two wretched boys. And in fact the fire brigade was successful only because the little Witch had released Fritz and Sepp from the spell just in time.

The Witches' Council

The witches' year was coming slowly to an end. Walpurgis Night drew nearer and nearer. Things were getting serious for the little Witch now. She was giving everything she had learnt a thorough revision these days. Once again she went through the Book of Witchcraft, page by page. She had her witchcraft at her fingertips.

Three days before Walpurgis Night Aunt Rumpumpel came riding along. She climbed down out of her black cloud to say, 'The Head Witch has told me to come and summon you before the Witches' Council. The test is at midnight the day after tomorrow. You're to be at the crossroads behind the red stone on the heath. However, if you've thought better of it, you don't *have* to come . . .'

'But I've got nothing to worry about!' said the little Witch.

'Who knows?' replied the witch Rumpumpel, shrugging her shoulders. 'It might be wiser to stay at home, all the same. I'd willingly make your excuses to the Head Witch.'

'Yes, I'm sure you would!' said the little Witch. 'But I'm not so stupid as you think. You can't frighten me.'

'There's no helping those who won't take advice!' said Aunt Rumpumpel. 'Well, till the day after tomorrow, then.'

Abraxas the raven would very much have liked to go with the little Witch this time. But he had no business

at the Witches' Council. He had to stay at home. When the little Witch set off he wished her the best of luck.

'Don't be nervous!' he called as they parted. 'You've been a good witch, that's the main thing.'

The little Witch reached the crossroads behind the red stone on the heath at the stroke of twelve. The Witches' Council was already assembled. Besides the Head Witch, there was a wind-witch, a wood-witch, a mist-witch, and one each of all the other kinds of witches. The storm-witches had sent Aunt Rumpumpel. But the little Witch was not afraid. She was sure of herself. 'She'll burst with fury when I pass the test and join the dance on the Brocken mountain tomorrow,' she thought.

'Let's begin,' said the Head Witch. 'Let's see what the little Witch has learned.'

So each in turn the witches set her exercises – calling up winds, and thunder, making the red stone on the heath disappear, conjuring up hail and rain. They were not particularly difficult questions. The little Witch was never once at a loss. Even when Aunt Rumpumpel told her, 'Cast the spell on page three hundred and twenty-four in the Book of Witchcraft!' she was not stuck for a moment. She knew the Book of Witchcraft inside out.

'By all means!' she said calmly, and she cast the spell on page three hundred and twenty-four in the

Book of Witchcraft – it was a thunderstorm with flashes of lightning.

'That will do!' said the Head Witch. 'You've shown us that you can cast spells. So in future I will let you join the dance on Walpurgis Night, although you're still rather young. Do any of the witches disagree?'

The other witches agreed with her. But Aunt Rumpumpel replied, 'I do.'

'What's your objection?' asked the Head Witch. 'Aren't you satisfied with her knowledge of witchcraft then?'

'No, it's not that,' said Aunt Rumpumpel. 'But she's a bad witch all the same. I can prove it!' She took a notebook out of her apron pocket. 'I've been watching her secretly all the year. I've written down the things she did. I'll read them out.'

'Read them out and welcome!' cried the little Witch. 'I've nothing to fear if it's not all a parcel of lies!'

'That remains to be seen!' said Aunt Rumpumpel. Then she read aloud to the Witches' Council what the little Witch had done during the year. She told them how she had helped the women picking up firewood, and how she had given the mean forester a lesson. And she told the stories of the flower-girl, the driver of the cart with the beer barrels, and the chestnut-man too. She told them about Corbinian the ox, whose life the little Witch had saved, and about the snowman and the boys who stole birds' eggs.

'Don't forget the tile-maker!' said the little Witch. 'I taught him a lesson too!'

She had expected Aunt Rumpumpel to take great pains to run her down. Instead, she was reading only her good deeds out of the notebook.

'Is this true?' asked the Head Witch after each story.

'Yes, it's quite true!' said the little Witch – and she felt proud of it.

In her pleasure, she never noticed that the Head Witch was putting her question in a sterner voice each time. Nor did she see the other witches shaking their heads more and more seriously. So she was terribly startled when the Head Witch suddenly cried in horror,

'And for two pins I'd have let *her* dance on the Brocken mountain tomorrow night! Ugh! ratsbane! What a bad witch!'

'But why?' asked the little Witch in surprise. 'I never did anything but good magic.'

'Exactly!' spat the Head Witch. 'The only good witches are those who do bad magic, bad magic all the time! But you kept on doing good things. You're a bad witch.'

'And what's more,' Aunt Rumpumpel told them, 'what's more, she once cast spells on a Friday! She did

it behind closed shutters, to be sure, but I was watching down the chimney.'

'What!' cried the Head Witch. 'This is the last straw!'

She seized the little Witch in her bony fingers and pulled her hair. At that all the other witches fell on the poor thing with wild shrieks and beat her with their broomsticks. They would have beaten the little

Witch till she was crooked and lame, if the Head Witch hadn't called, after a while,

'That's enough now! I know a better punishment for her.'

'You shall collect the wood for the witches' bonfire on the Brocken mountain,' she told the little Witch spitefully. 'All by yourself. By midnight tomorrow you must have the bonfire built. Then we shall tie you to a tree near by, and you shall stand and watch the rest of us dancing all night long!'

'And when we've had a dance or two, suggested Aunt Rumpumpel, 'we'll go and tear the hairs from her head. One by one! That will be fun – we shall enjoy that! She won't forget this Walpurgis Night for a long time.'

She who laughs last . . .

'Miserable raven that I am!' groaned good old Abraxas when the little Witch had told him what had happened at the crossroads behind the red stone on the heath. 'It's my fault, all my fault! I was the one who told you to keep doing good magic. Oh, if only I could at least help you!'

'I must do it by myself,' said the little Witch. 'I'm not sure how just yet . . . But I shan't let myself be tied to a tree, I know that much!'

She ran indoors and took the Book of Witchcraft out of the table drawer. She began turning the pages fast.

'Will you take me with you?' asked Abraxas.

'Where?'

'To the Brocken mountain! I don't want to leave you alone tonight.'

'All right,' said the little Witch. 'I'll take you with me. But only on one condition; you must keep your beak shut now and not disturb me.'

Abraxas kept quiet. The little Witch buried herself in the Book of Witchcraft. From time to time she

muttered something. The raven didn't understand,
but he took care not to ask questions.

This went on until evening. Then the little Witch
stood up and said,

'I've got it now! Let's ride to the Brocken mountain!'

As yet there was no sign of the other witches on the Brocken mountain. They had to wait for the hour of midnight before they could mount their broomsticks and ride there. That was the custom for witches on Walpurgis Night.

The little Witch sat down on top of the mountain and stretched her legs out in front of her.

'Aren't you going to start?' asked Abraxas.

'Start?' said the little Witch. 'Start what?'

'Collecting wood! Aren't you supposed to be building a bonfire?'

'Plenty of time!' said the little Witch, smiling.

'But there's only an hour left before midnight,' replied Abraxas. 'It's just struck eleven down in the valley.'

'It can strike half past too,' said the little Witch. 'Don't worry, the bonfire will be ready on time.'

'Let's hope so!' croaked Abraxas. The little Witch's calm was beginning to make him feel uneasy. If only everything turned out all right!

Down in the valley it struck half-past eleven.

'Hurry up!' Abraxas urged her. 'Only half an hour left.'

'Quarter of an hour is long enough for me,' she answered obstinately.

When it struck quarter to twelve, she sprang to her feet. 'Now to collect the wood!' she cried, and she repeated a magic spell.

They came flying up from all directions, cracking and snapping and clattering. They fell helter-skelter, piling up on top of each other into a heap.

'Aha!' cried Abraxas. 'What do I see? Aren't those broomsticks?'

'Yes, they're broomsticks – they're the big witches' broomsticks! I'm casting a spell to bring them all to the Brocken. And that one, the long one there, is the Head Witch's broomstick.'

'What – what does it mean?' asked Abraxas the raven in alarm.

'I'm going to set them alight,' said the little Witch. 'They'll burn well, don't you think? But I still need paper for the fire.'

She repeated a second spell.

Now a rushing and blustering noise rose in the air. They came flying over the woods to the mountain top, like troops of giant bats, beating their wings.

'Come along!' cried the little Witch. 'Quick! Up on the pile of broomsticks.'

They were the big witches' Book of Witchcraft. The little Witch had ordered them to fly to the Brocken.

'What are you doing!' croaked Abraxas. 'The big witches will kill you!'

'I don't think so,' said the little Witch, and she recited a third spell.

This was the most powerful spell of all. It took

away all the big witches' witchcraft. Not one of them could work magic any more. And as they had lost their Books of Witchcraft too, they would never be able to learn it again.

Down in the valley midnight struck.

'There!' cried the little Witch happily. 'Now we'll begin! Hurrah for Walpurgis Night!'

She set fire to the broomsticks and the Books of Witchcraft with the firework she had bought from Jacob Cheapjack.

It was the most beautiful bonfire you can imagine. The flames shot up towards the sky, hissing and crackling.

And the little Witch, alone with Abraxas the raven, danced round the blazing bonfire till morning. Now she was the only witch in the world who could work magic. Yesterday the other witches had laughed her to scorn. It was her turn now.

'Walpurgis Night!' the little Witch cried happily on top of the Brocken.

'Hurrah for Walpurgis Night!'

Also published by Knight Books

Otfried Preussler

THE LITTLE GHOST

The little ghost lived in an old oak chest in
a cobwebbed corner of an attic in an
old castle. He was one of those harmless
ghosts who haunt places by night, and never
hurt anyone unless they are provoked. He
enjoyed haunting, but did so wish he could see
the town by day instead of by night. Then
one day it happened. But a town by
daylight is no place for a little white ghost.

Post·A·Book

A Royal Mail service in association with the Book Marketing Council & The Booksellers Association.

Post-A-Book is a Post Office trademark.